The KnowHow Book of Jokes and Tricks

Heather Amery and Ian Adair

Illustrated by Colin King
Designed by John Jamieson

WHY DO BIRDS FLY SOUTH IN THE AUTUMN?

WHAT IS YELLOW AND VERY DANGEROUS?

SHARK-INFESTED CUSTARD!

BECAUSE IT IS TOO FAR TO WALK!

WHY DO BEES HUM?

Contents

BECAUSE THEY DON'T KNOW THE WORDS!

WHAT DO YOU GET IF YOU CROSS A KANGAROO WITH A SHEEP?

A WOOLLY JUMPER!

WHY DO COWS WEAR BELLS?

BECAUSE THEIR HORNS DON'T WORK!

Special Contributor:
Peter Howarth

Cover Illustration:
Neil Ross

Usborne Publishing Ltd
Usborne House
83-85 Saffron Hill, London EC1N 8RT

Printed in Italy

About This Book

This book is for everyone who likes tricks, magic, conjuring, surprises and jokes. It is full of magic secrets on how to do very quick, easy tricks as well as more difficult ones which need lots and lots of practice.

At the end of the book are five special pages about putting on a show for your friends. They tell you how to be a real magician and how to make the things you will need.

There are lots of things you can make for magic tricks and surprises. All you need are cardboard boxes, bottle tops, matchboxes, string, glue, paper, paint and a pack of playing cards.

You will also need a big box to keep all your magic in. Magicians always keep their tricks a secret and never tell anyone how they do them. You will have to keep this book secret, too.

With the startling and surprising tricks, be careful who you play them on. Some grown-ups may not think they are funny if you give them a nasty shock.

Tips and Hints

All the best tricks look like magic because of the way you do them. All your movements should be very big and impressive. Stare at what you are doing and pretend you can really do magic.

The important thing is to practise all the tricks lots of times in secret. Then when you do them in front of people, they will look like real magic.

It helps a trick if you say some magic words. We have made up some special ones. They are ZIXEE SOXEE ZABADEE ZUT but you can make up your own if you like. Try to think of funny words which are not real words but sound magical.

Remember never to do the same trick twice in front of the same people – even if they beg you. If you do, they may guess how you do it and spoil the magic. The best magic is secret.

Making a Magic Wand

A wand is a useful thing to have when you do magic tricks. You can wave it when you say the magic words or push it through things to show they are empty.

You can buy a wand from a magic shop or make one of your own. Here are two easy ways of making wands. The wooden one will, of course, last much longer.

If you point your wand at something, the people watching will look at it. Then you can do a trick without them noticing the secret part.

Paper Wand

Cut out an oblong of stiff black paper, or paper painted black, about 30 cm long and 10 cm wide. Roll it round two pencils (a) and glue the edge to make a tube.

When the glue is dry, shake out the pencils. Cut two strips of white paper, each about 2 cm wide and 8 cm long. Glue one to each end of the wand, like this, (b).

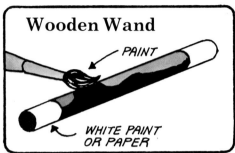

Wooden Wand

To make a wooden wand, you need a piece of thin stick or dowel, about 30 cm long. Paint it black or glue on black paper. Paint the ends white or glue on white paper.

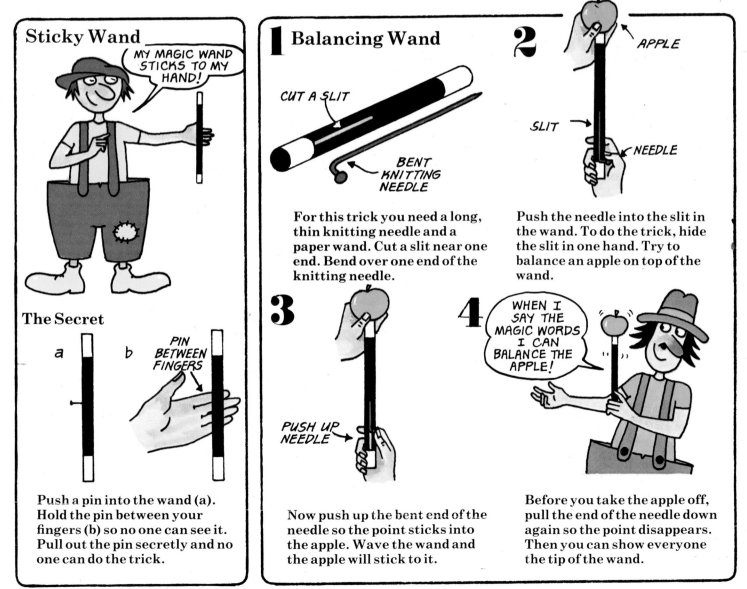

Sticky Wand

MY MAGIC WAND STICKS TO MY HAND!

The Secret

a   b   PIN BETWEEN FINGERS

Push a pin into the wand (a). Hold the pin between your fingers (b) so no one can see it. Pull out the pin secretly and no one can do the trick.

1 Balancing Wand

CUT A SLIT

BENT KNITTING NEEDLE

For this trick you need a long, thin knitting needle and a paper wand. Cut a slit near one end. Bend over one end of the knitting needle.

2

APPLE

SLIT

NEEDLE

Push the needle into the slit in the wand. To do the trick, hide the slit in one hand. Try to balance an apple on top of the wand.

3

PUSH UP NEEDLE

Now push up the bent end of the needle so the point sticks into the apple. Wave the wand and the apple will stick to it.

4

WHEN I SAY THE MAGIC WORDS I CAN BALANCE THE APPLE!

Before you take the apple off, pull the end of the needle down again so the point disappears. Then you can show everyone the tip of the wand.

Table Tricks

Here are some good tricks you can play while you are sitting at a table having a meal.

For the Table Napkin Creepy You will need
an empty cotton reel
a candle
a table knife
a strong rubber band
a thin stick, about 10 cm long
a small paper table napkin
scissors
a matchstick and sticky tape

1 Table Napkin Creepy

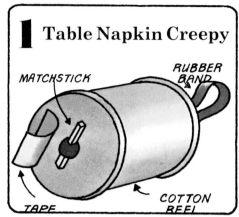

Push the rubber band through the cotton reel. Push a bit of match stick through the loop at one end. Stick the match stick to the reel with a bit of tape.

2

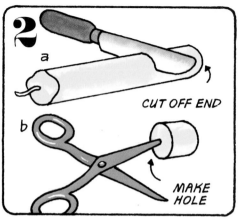

Cut a ring, about 1 cm wide, off the end of a candle with a table knife. Make a hole through the middle with scissors.

3

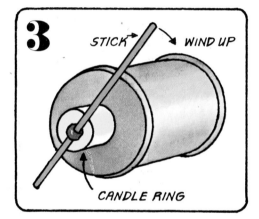

Push the free end of the rubber band through the candle ring. Then push the stick through the loop. Wind the stick round about 20 times.

4

Put the cotton reel on the table when no one is looking. Drop a small table napkin over it. Leave it to creep along very slowly. Someone will soon notice it.

5

To make an even creepier Creepy, cut a circle, about the size of a saucer, out of very thin black cloth. Snip the edges all the way round. Put it over the cotton reel.

Floating Sugar Lumps

Cut out a neat square from a piece of white plastic sponge. Put it in a bowl of sugar lumps. When someone drops it into a cup of tea or coffee, it will float.

Empty Spoon

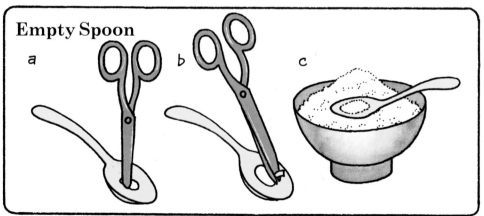

Make a hole in the bowl of a plastic spoon with scissors, like this (a). Cut out a big hole as neatly as you can (b) with scissors.

Put the spoon down on some sugar in a basin (c). It will look as if it has sugar in it. Anyone trying to spoon up the sugar will get a surprise.

Which English king invented the fireplace? Alfred the Grate!

Ready-Sliced Banana

1 How It Looks

HERE IS AN ORDINARY BANANA.

2 WITH MY MAGIC WAND I SLICE IT IN BITS WITHOUT CUTTING THE SKIN.

3 WHEN I PEEL THE BANANA IT IS SLICED INTO BITS!

The Secret

a BIG NEEDLE THREAD

b

c

d

Push a piece of strong thread, about 20 cm long, through the eye of a big needle. Push the needle through one flat side of a big banana (a).

Pull the needle out, leaving the thread under the skin. Now push the needle back through the same hole and under the next flat side (b). Do this all round the skin (c).

When you get round to the first hole, pull the two ends of the thread. This will cut the banana inside the skin. Make more cuts down the banana inside the skin (d).

Magic Straw

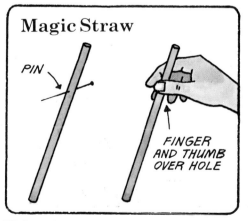

PIN

FINGER AND THUMB OVER HOLE

Make a hole in a drinking straw with a pin. When someone tries to drink with it, they will just suck up air. When you drink with it, put your fingers over the holes.

Why do witches fly about on broomsticks?

Singing Glasses

a   b

You can make a glass sing a long whining tune. Just put a little water in the glass. Dip one finger in the water and rub it gently round the top edge of the glass (a).

If it does not work at once, try rubbing harder or more gently. Keep your finger just on the rim (b). Thin glasses work better than thick ones. Try lots of different ones.

Because vacuum cleaners are too heavy!

Finger Tricks

These Finger Tricks are great fun to do. When you play them, you can pretend you are hurt. With the Wounded Finger, just wear the bandage until someone notices. Then pretend you are very brave.

The Wand Through Head Trick needs a bit of practicing. Try it secretly in front of a mirror until it looks right. You can pull the wand out of your head again. Just hold the wand in place with your other hand. Then slide the paper back along the wand.

Wounded Finger

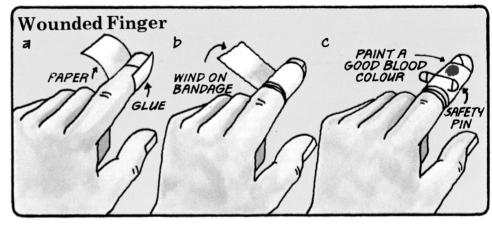

Wrap a piece of white paper round one finger (a). Stick it with glue. Wind on a short piece of bandage, going over the top of the finger as well (b). Pin the end.

Paint one bit of bandage a good red colour. Put on a bit of brown to look like dried blood (c). Slide off the bandage. Put it on secretly before you fool someone.

Which Wounded Finger?

Make a Wounded Finger bandage just big enough to go on the top of one finger (a). To change it to another finger, bend the finger over into your palm (b).

Hold the bandage with your thumb and slide it off (c). Slide the bandage on to the next finger. Open your hand to show that a different finger is hurt (d).

Practise sliding the bandage off and on quickly. You can move it to all your fingers, one at a time. Pretend you cannot remember which finger has the wound.

Shaky Hand

Hold out your hand to shake hands with someone. When they take it, off it comes.

The Secret

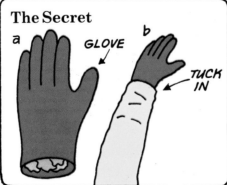

Stuff the fingers and palm of a glove with paper tissues or bits of rag. Make sure the fingers look full and fat (a). Hold the glove by the open end. Pull down your sleeve to hide your hand (b).

Missing Finger

Pull on a woollen glove, putting two fingers into one space. This leaves an empty glove finger which you can wiggle about in a horrible floppy way.

Which trees do fingers and thumbs grow on? Palm trees!

6

1 Living Finger

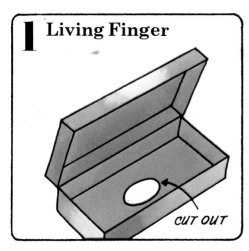

CUT OUT

Find a small cardboard cigar or chocolate box with a hinged lid. Cut a hole, big enough for your finger to go through, in the bottom of the box.

2

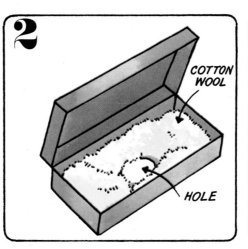

COTTON WOOL

HOLE

Glue cotton wool to the bottom of the box. Put it round the hole but not over it. Close the box before you show anyone the Finger.

3

Hold the box in one hand, like this. Then, as you open the box, quickly push one finger through the hole and bend it over. Keep it still and then wiggle it.

String Through Finger Trick

IT DOESN'T HURT MUCH IF I DO IT SLOWLY!

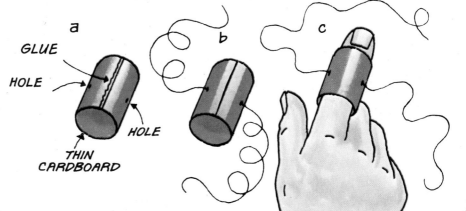

a

GLUE

HOLE

THIN CARDBOARD

HOLE

b

c

Cut out a piece of thin cardboard about 7 cm long and 4 cm wide. Roll it into a tube and glue the edges together (a). Make a hole in each side of the tube.

Push a piece of string, about 50 cm long, through the holes (b). Slide the tube on to one finger (c). Slowly pull one end of the string. Then pull the other end.

Wand Through Head Trick

Before You Start

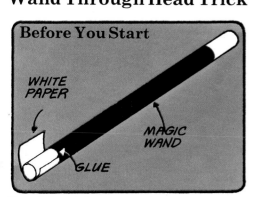

WHITE PAPER

MAGIC WAND

GLUE

For this trick you need a black wand with white ends. You also need to wear long sleeves. Wrap a bit of white paper round one end of the wand. Glue down the end.

1

Hold the end of the wand which has the paper on it. Put the other end to your head, behind one ear. Make sure the back of your hand is towards the people watching you.

2

Now push the bit of paper very slowly along the wand so that the wand looks as if it is going into your head. The end in your hand slides up your sleeve.

What's worse than a giraffe with a sore throat?   A centipede with sore feet!

7

Disappearing and Appearing Tricks

Vanishing Water

Make this magazine a magic one and use it to make water vanish. When you have done the trick, put the magazine down so it is upright and pour out the water when no one is looking. You can use the magazine lots of times for making other things appear or disappear.

The magazine should be thick but floppy and make sure there are no holes in the plastic bag.

Before You Start

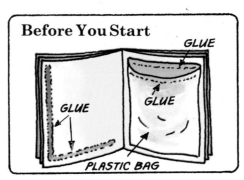

Spread glue on the top edges of a small plastic bag. Press the bag to an inside page of a magazine. Close the magazine and press the pages together. Leave to dry.

1 How It Looks

HERE IS AN ORDINARY MAGAZINE. YOU CAN SEE THE INSIDE AND THE OUTSIDE.

2 I ROLL IT INTO A CONE AND STIR IT WITH MY MAGIC WAND.

1 The Secret

OPEN THE BAG WITH WAND

Roll the magazine into a cone. Push one end of a magic wand into the pages where the plastic bag is. Waggle the wand round to open the top of the bag, like this.

3 I POUR IN SOME WATER AND SAY THE MAGIC WORDS.

2

POUR WATER INTO BAG

Pour about half a cup of water into the bag. If you pour in just a very little and then a bit more and then a bit more, it will look like quite a lot of water.

4 I UNROLL THE MAGAZINE AND THE WATER HAS DISAPPEARED!

3 HOLD UP MAGAZINE

Unroll the magazine and hold it up by the top corners. Show the inside and outside. Close it and put it down so it stands upright or the water will run out.

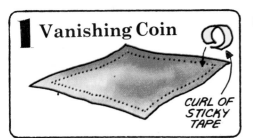

1 Vanishing Coin

CURL OF STICKY TAPE

Make a small curl of sticky tape, like this, so the sticky side is outside. Press it down in the corner of a small scarf or coloured handkerchief.

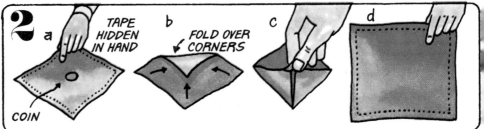

2 a TAPE HIDDEN IN HAND b FOLD OVER CORNERS c d

COIN

Cover the sticky tape with one hand and ask someone to put a small coin on the scarf (a). Fold over the corner and press the tape down on to the coin (b).

Fold over the other three corners, like this (c). Pick up the first corner, covering the coin with your hand (d). Show that the coin has disappeared from the scarf.

What sort of lighting did Noah put in the Ark? ¡Flood lighting!

Empty Tube

Use a big empty tube to make things appear out of the air. This trick cannot be done too close to other people or they will see how it works. When you have finished the trick, stand the tube up on end so no one can see where things come from.

You will need

2 sheets of stiff black paper, or paper painted black, about 25 cm long and 25 cm wide
glue
coloured tissues or thin paper

1 **How It Looks**

HERE IS AN ABSOLUTELY EMPTY TUBE. YOU CAN SEE THERE IS NOTHING IN IT.

2

I SAY THE MAGIC WORDS AND SUDDENLY, LOTS OF THINGS APPEAR!

1 **Before You Start**

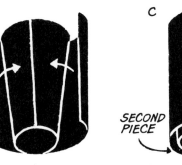

a
GLUE EDGE

b

c
GLUE EDGE AND CUT ROUND

SECOND PIECE

Roll one piece of black paper into a tube. Make it slightly wider at one end (a). Stick the edge with glue. Spread glue round the top of the wider end.

Wrap the second piece of paper round the first tube (b). Glue the edges exactly together to make the second tube straight. Cut off the bits at the top (c).

2

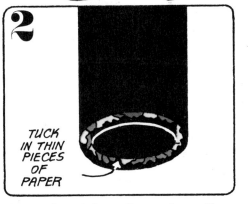

TUCK IN THIN PIECES OF PAPER

To get the trick ready, push small bits of coloured tissue or thin paper down between the two tubes. Hold this end towards you so no one can see the secret space.

1 **Making Biscuits**

a   GLUE

b   THIN BISCUITS

Open a thick, floppy magazine or comic in the middle. Glue the pages together on each side and bottom (a). When the glue is dry, put some biscuits in one side (b).

2

a   b

To do the trick, let everyone see you put some things, like bits of coloured paper and pencils, into the magazine. Close the magazine.

Now say the magic words or wave your wand. Open the magazine again and tip out the biscuits. Be careful to hold the other side so the things do not drop out.

What's green, hairy and goes up and down? A gooseberry in a lift!

Cutting and Mending Magic

Here are two easy ways to cut string in half and then make it into one piece again. All you need are pieces of string and a pair of scissors.

For the Tearing Trick, you will need two small paper handkerchiefs, which look exactly alike, and some glue.

When you do the tricks, look at your hands as if you really expect some magic to happen. And remember to say the magic words each time.

Short Cut

1 How It Looks

HERE IS A PERFECTLY ORDINARY PIECE OF STRING. I CUT IT IN HALF.

I SAY THE MAGIC WORDS AND IT IS IN ONE PIECE AGAIN!

2

1 The Secret

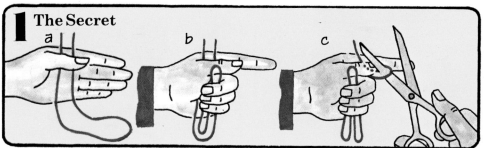

Hold the ends of the string in one hand (a). Bring up the loop and hold it with your fingers (b).

Hook one blade of the scissors under one string near the end (c). Pretend you are hooking the loop.

2

Pull the string up above your hand so it can be seen. Cut the string very slowly and obviously.

3

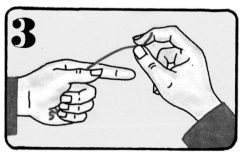

Hold one bit of the string you have cut. Push all the rest of the string into your hand and hold it.

4

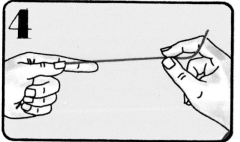

Say the magic words. Pull the string very slowly out of your hand to show it is in one piece.

5

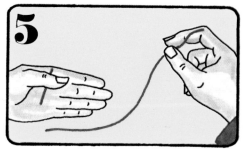

Keep the short cut-off string in your hand. Hide it in your pocket when no one is looking.

1 String Along

SMALL LOOP

Hide a short loop of string in your hand (a). Let everyone see you hold a long piece (b).

2

Hook one blade of the scissors under the short loop and pull it up a bit. Cut it in half.

3

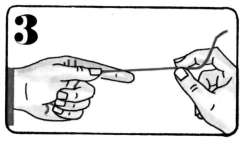

Push all the string into your hand. Hold one end of the long piece and pull it out. Hide the short bits.

What is an astronaut's watch called? A lunartick!

10

Tearing Trick

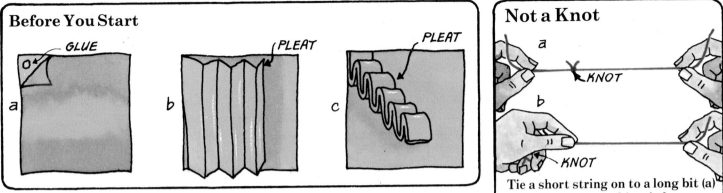

Before You Start

Put two paper handkerchiefs, which look exactly the same, on top of each other. Drop a bit of glue on to one corner (a) and stick them together.

Fold the top hanky backwards and forwards to pleat it into a strip (b). Pleat the strip (c) to make a neat square in one corner. The trick is now ready.

Not a Knot

Tie a short string on to a long bit (a) so it looks like two bits tied together. Put all the string in one hand. Pull out one end, sliding the knot along and hiding it in your hand (b). The knot has vanished.

How It Looks

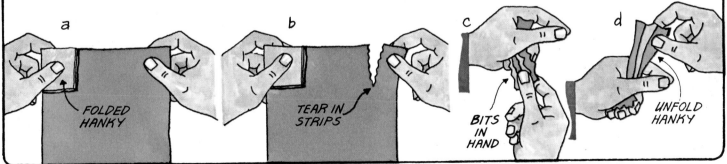

The Secret

Hold the paper handkerchief in one hand with your thumb over the folded-up one (a). Hold the top of the hanky with the other hand and tear it into strips (b).

Tear the strips into bits. Put all the bits into one hand (c). Hold your hand up to your mouth and whisper the magic words.

Take hold of the top corner of the folded-up hanky. Pull it slowly out of your hand so it unfolds (d). Hide the torn-up bits in your other hand so no one sees them.

If pig skins make good shoes, what do banana skins make? Good slippers!

Matchbox Magic
Small Change

1

HERE IS AN EMPTY MATCHBOX.

1 The Secret — MATCHBOX TRAY — CUT OUT

Take the tray out of the box. Cut a narrow slit in the bottom of one end of the tray.

2

JUST DROP IN A VERY SMALL COIN.

2 a — BIG COIN
b — COIN HERE

Hold a big coin on the tray (a). Push the tray into the cover so the coin is held inside (b).

3

I CLOSE THE BOX, OPEN IT AGAIN AND TIP OUT A BIG COIN!

3 DROP IN SMALL COIN

Show someone that the box is empty and ask them to drop in a small coin.

4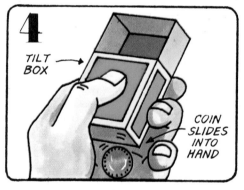

TILT BOX — COIN SLIDES INTO HAND

Tilt the box so the small coin slides out of the slit in the tray and into your hand.

5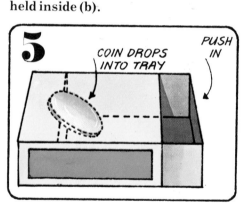

COIN DROPS INTO TRAY — PUSH IN

Push in the tray. The big coin drops into the tray. Hide the small coin in your hand.

6

OPEN BOX TO SHOW COIN

Say the magic words. Open the matchbox again and tip out the big coin into your empty hand.

Obedient Matchbox

JUST CALL 'STOP' AND I WILL STOP THE MATCHBOX ANYWHERE ON THE STRING!

Hold the string with the box loosely. The box will slide down. When it reaches the end, hold the string up the other way. To stop the box, pull the string tight.

Before You Start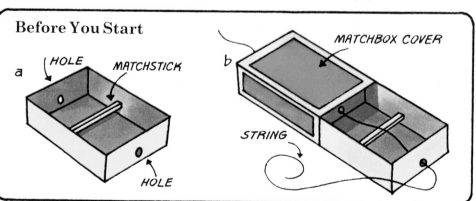

a — HOLE — MATCHSTICK — HOLE
b — MATCHBOX COVER — STRING

Take the tray out of a matchbox. Make a hole in each end of the tray. Break one end off a matchstick so it just fits into the tray. Jam it into the tray.

Push a piece of string through one hole, over the matchstick and out through the other hole. Slide on the matchbox cover (b).

What's a good place for water skiing? A sloping lake!

More Matches

1 HERE IS A FULL BOX OF MATCHES.

For this trick you need a box of safety matches which looks exactly the same on both sides of the box.

2 I SHAKE OUT ALL THE MATCHES.

Hold your hand over the box so that no one can see the other side.

3 I OPEN THE BOX AGAIN, AND IT'S FULL OF MATCHES!

Close the box and secretly turn it over in your hand. Do not shake it or the matches will rattle.

---

1 Before You Start

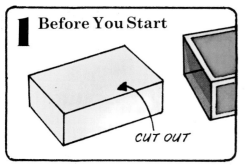

CUT OUT

Take the tray out of the box. Cut out the bottom very neatly. Pull off any bits of paper.

2

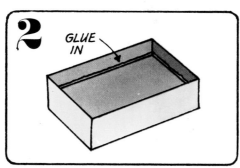

GLUE IN

Push the bottom half-way up into the tray. Glue it all the way round. Leave the glue dry.

3

Fill one side of the box with matches. Turn the box over and fill up the other side.

Colour Changes

You can use the More Matches box to do other tricks. Here is a simple one. You can probably think of some of your own to do.

Remember never to let anyone look very closely at the box or they will see how you do the tricks.

1

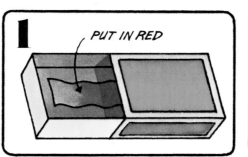

PUT IN RED

Before you start, put a piece of blue paper or cloth in one side of the box. Turn the box over. Show that it is empty. Put in some red paper or a bit of cloth.

2

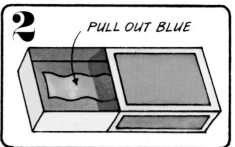

PULL OUT BLUE

Close the box and secretly turn it over. You can do this by waving it about and saying the magic words. Open the box and the red paper or cloth has turned blue.

Rattling Boxes

1

HERE IS A FULL BOX OF MATCHES. I CLOSE THE BOX AND SHAKE IT BUT IT DOESN'T RATTLE!

2

HERE IS AN EMPTY BOX. I CLOSE IT AND SHAKE IT. STRANGE, IT DOES RATTLE!

The Secret

For this trick you need three boxes of safety matches – one full box, a half-full one and an empty one. Jam some extra matches into the full one so the box does not rattle when you shake it.

Put the half-full box up your left sleeve and hold it there with an elastic band round your arm. When you shake the empty box, the box up your sleeve makes the rattling noise. When you shake the full box, make sure you hold it in your right hand or the one up your sleeve will rattle.

What has a bottom at its top? A leg!

13

Jack-in-the-Tube

Push down the head of this jack-in-the-tube and leave it to pop up again. If it takes a long time to jump, tap it very gently on the end.

You will need
3 small cardboard tubes
a ping pong ball
5 long, thin rubber bands
2 long, big-headed pins
sticky tape and scissors
thin paper and paints

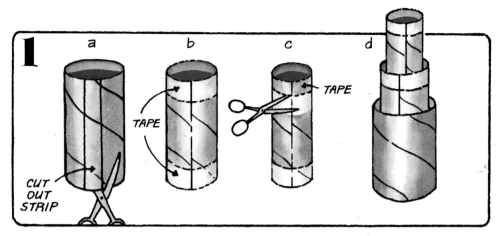

Cut a strip, about 1 cm wide, out of a cardboard tube (a). Hold the cut edges together and stick them with tape (b).

Cut a strip, about 2 cm wide, out of a second tube. Stick it with tape. Cut about 2 cm off the top (c). Put the three tubes together (d) to make sure they slide easily.

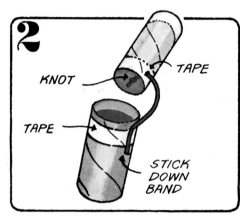

Make a hole in one side of the smallest tube. Cut a rubber band in half. Push one end through the hole and tie a knot. Tape the other end to the second tube.

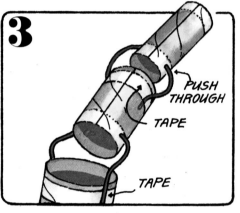

Join the second tube to the third tube in the same way. Now join the other sides of each tube with rubber bands. The tubes should be about 2 cm apart.

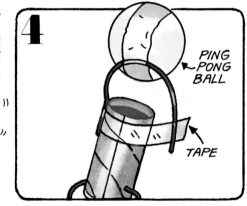

Cut another rubber band in half. Tape it to the top of the smallest tube with tape. Tape the ping pong ball to the rubber band.

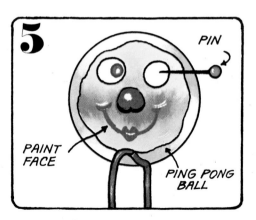

Push pins into the ping pong ball for the eyes. Paint or colour the face. Paint the tubes or cover them with coloured paper.

Man: Hey, you're not allowed to fish in that river.
Boy: I'm not fishing. I'm teaching my pet worm to swim!

14

Squirting Flower

Put this flower in your button hole. When someone is close enough, squeeze the tube to make it squirt water.

You will need
an empty plastic tube with a
    screw-on top
a plastic drinking straw
a coloured plastic bag
a paper clip
waterproof glue, such as Bostick 1
thin thread
scissors

WOULD YOU LIKE TO SMELL THIS LOVELY SCENT?

WOULD YOU LIKE TO SMELL MY PLASTIC FLOWER?

1

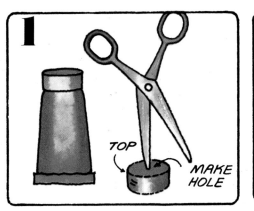

TOP   MAKE HOLE

Take the top off the plastic tube. Make a small hole in the top with scissors, like this.

2

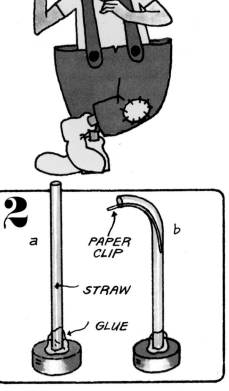

a   b

PAPER CLIP

STRAW

GLUE

Push one end of a plastic straw into the hole. Glue it to the top (a). Straighten out a paper clip. Bend over one end and push it into the top of the straw (b).

Scent Bottle

a

PLASTIC BOTTLE

MAKE HOLES

Make about six small holes in the bottom of an empty plastic bottle with one blade of the scissors, like this.

b

PUT ON TOP

FILL WITH WATER

3

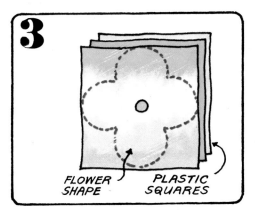

FLOWER SHAPE   PLASTIC SQUARES

Cut three squares from a plastic bag. Put them together and cut out a flower petal shape, like this. Cut a small hole in the middle of each shape.

4

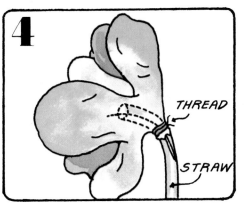

THREAD

STRAW

Push the top of the straw through the holes in the flower shapes. Tie them to the straw with thread. Pour some water into the plastic tube and screw on the top.

Fill the bottle to the top with water. Screw on the lid very quickly. No water will come out if you hold the bottle upright. But when someone takes off the lid, just watch . . .

What was purple and tried to conquer the world? Alexander the Grape!

Puzzlers

Magic Seesaw

Set up this seesaw and make it go up and down as many times as you like. Be careful not to touch the cups as you do it.

You will need

a strong ruler or flat piece of wood about 35 cm long

2 empty yoghurt pots or paper cups

a matchbox

a jug of water

Before You Start

Put the middle of the ruler on the matchbox, like this. Put a pot or cup on each one. Make sure they balance each other exactly.

How It Looks

1 I PUT MY FINGER IN ONE POT AND THE SEESAW GOES DOWN. WHEN I TAKE IT OUT AND PUT IT IN THE OTHER THE SEESAW TIPS THE OTHER WAY.

2 I POUR THE WATER OUT OF THE TWO POTS. NOW COMES THE DIFFICULT PART.

3 IF I TRY VERY HARD I CAN MAKE THE SEESAW GO DOWN WITHOUT TOUCHING THE POTS. IT'S VERY DIFFICULT TO DO. I HAVE TO GET VERY CLOSE AND THINK HARD AT ONE END AND THEN THE OTHER.

The Secret

When you dip your finger into the water in a cup, the seesaw goes down. Anyone can do this. When you put your finger in an empty cup, bend down very close to it and pretend to try very hard. Then groan a little as if it is difficult. When you groan, blow gently into the cup and it will go down. Then groan and blow gently into the other cup. Be careful not to touch the cups. This looks like real magic.

Spooky Straws

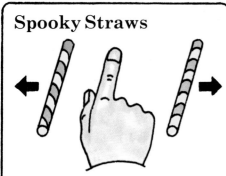

Cut a drinking straw in half. Put the bits down, like this. When you put a finger between them and say the magic words, they move apart. When you speak, blow gently at the same time down your finger.

Linking Clips

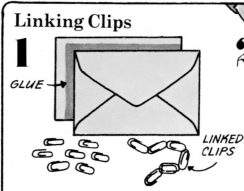

1 GLUE   LINKED CLIPS

For this trick, find two envelopes which look the same. Glue them back to back. Link up seven paper clips and drop them into one of the envelopes. Close both flaps.

2 To do the trick, open the empty envelope. Drop in seven clips and close the flap. Secretly turn the envelopes over, saying the magic words. Open the flap and tip out the linked clips.

If a buttercup is yellow, what colour is a hiccup?   Burple!

Paper Chase

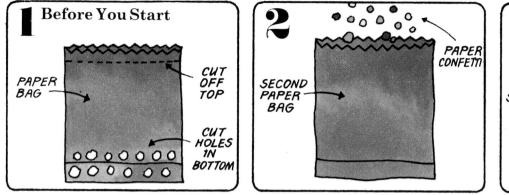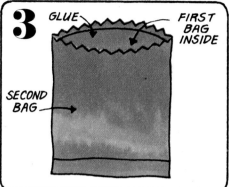

1. Before You Start

PAPER BAG
CUT OFF TOP
CUT HOLES IN BOTTOM

Find two small paper bags which are the same size and colour. Cut about 1 cm off the top of one bag. Cut some holes in the bottom of the bag, to let air through when you blow in it.

2.

PAPER CONFETTI
SECOND PAPER BAG

Cut up lots of bits of coloured paper to make confetti. Put the bits into the second paper bag. When you do the trick, this bag bursts but not the one with the holes in it.

3.

GLUE
FIRST BAG INSIDE
SECOND BAG

Push the first bag into the second one. Glue the edges of the two bags together round the tops. Make sure the inside bag is very smooth. When you have done the trick, quickly crumple up the bags.

1. How It Looks

THIS IS AN ORDINARY PAPER BAG. YOU CAN SEE IT IS EMPTY. I PUSH IN A COUPLE OF PAPER TISSUES.

2.

I BLOW UP THE BAG AND THEN SAY THE MAGIC WORDS.

3.

WHEN I BURST THE BAG THE TISSUES HAVE TURNED INTO COLOURED CONFETTI!

Knotty Problem

1.

WATCH ME TIE A KNOT IN THIS HANDKERCHIEF.

2.

I FLIP IT ONCE, TWICE AND A THIRD TIME AND THERE IS THE KNOT.

The Secret

a b c

Tie a knot in a corner of a hanky. Hide the knot in one hand (a). Flip the hanky upwards, twice (b). The third time, drop the knot and grab the other end (c). Practise until you can do this very quickly.

What are the best things to put into a fruit pie? ¡Your teeth!

Creepies and Crawlies

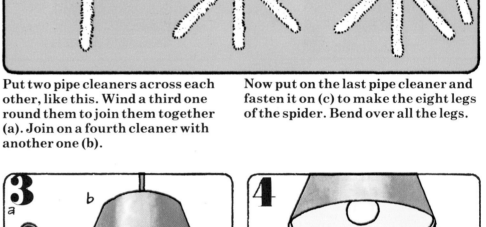

Climbing Spider

This monster spider climbs down its thread and up again. Hang it up in a dimly-lit room and no one will notice how you work it. The nastier it looks the bigger the horrible surprise.

You will need
6 pipe cleaners
cotton wool
2 small buttons and 2 pins
thin black thread
a paper clip
glue and black paint

1

Put two pipe cleaners across each other, like this. Wind a third one round them to join them together (a). Join on a fourth cleaner with another one (b).

Now put on the last pipe cleaner and fasten it on (c) to make the eight legs of the spider. Bend over all the legs.

2

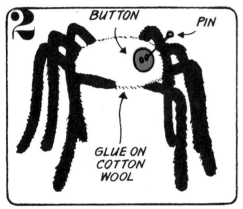

Glue a lump of cotton wool to the middle of the legs to make the body. Paint the whole thing black. Pin on two bright buttons to make the eyes.

3

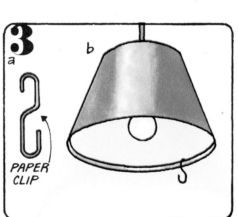

Bend a paper clip, like this, to make a loop at each end (a). Hook one end on to the frame of a lamp shade, on the inside (b).

4

Tie a very long piece of black thread to the top of the spider. Hook the thread over the paper clip. Pull the end of the thread to make the spider go up and down.

Crawlies

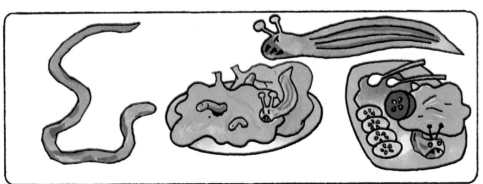

You can make lots of nasty crawlies out of coloured plasticine. Roll out a long pink bit to make a wriggly worm. Shape some brown plasticine to look like a slug, with bits for its horns. On a lettuce leaf or in a plate of salad these nasties will look quite real and will put anyone off their food.

Caterpillars

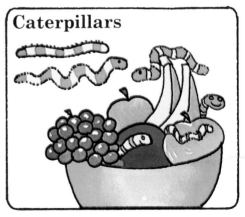

Cut a pipe cleaner into four bits to make caterpillars. Paint them yellowy green or in yellow and green stripes. When the paint is dry, bend them into wriggly shapes.

How do you know when it's raining cats and dogs?   When you step in a poodle!

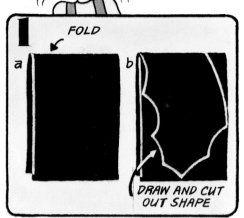
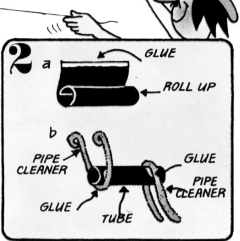

Flying Bat

This bat flies across a room at great speed. Make it look as horrible as you can. It will look best in a fairly dark room.

You will need

a sheet of stiff black paper, or white paper and black paint
a piece of black paper, about 8 cm long and 4 cm wide
2 pipe cleaners
a small curtain ring
very thin nylon string or fishing line, about 8 metres long
glue, sticky tape and scissors

1 FOLD / DRAW AND CUT OUT SHAPE

Fold the sheet of paper in half (a). Draw the shape of a bat's wing on one side (b). Cut out the shape but do not cut along the folded edge. Open out the paper.

2 GLUE / ROLL UP / PIPE CLEANER / GLUE / PIPE CLEANER / GLUE / TUBE

Roll up the small piece of paper to make a tube. Glue the edge (a). Bend a pipe cleaner round one end for the eyes and one round the other end for legs (b). Glue on.

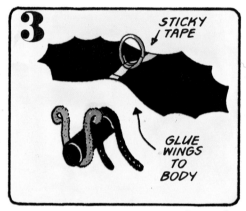

3 STICKY TAPE / GLUE WINGS TO BODY

Stick the curtain ring upright to the middle of the wings with tape. Glue the wings to the body, like this. Paint the pipe cleaners black and bend them a little.

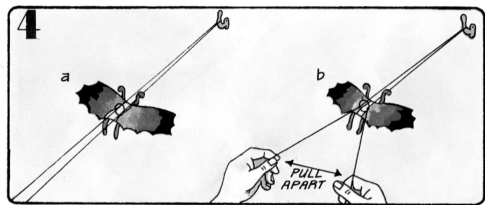

4 PULL APART

Hook the middle of the nylon string on to something high up in a room, perhaps near a door. Slide the ends of the string through the ring on the bat (a).

Hold one end of one string in each hand. Slide the bat down close to your hands. Now pull the strings apart as quickly as you can. The bat will fly along them (b).

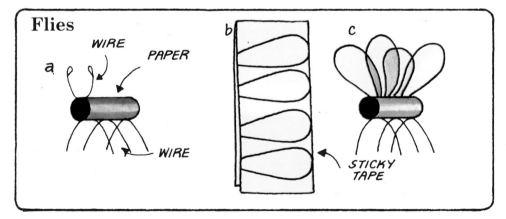

Flies

WIRE / PAPER / WIRE / STICKY TAPE

Make a little roll of paper and glue the edge. Cut some short bits of very thin wire. Glue them on to make legs and antennae (a). Paint the paper black. Leave to dry.

Fold over a piece of sticky tape so the sticky sides are together. Cut out four oval shapes (b) and glue them on as the fly's wings (c). Everyone hates flies.

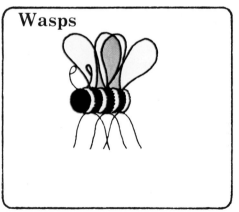

Wasps

Make another fly but before you glue on the wings, wind a pipe cleaner round the body. Paint it in yellow and black stripes. Then glue on the wings.

What did one eye say to the other eye? ¡sllǝws ʇɐɥʇ sn uǝǝʍʇǝq ǝɯoɔ sɐɥ ƃuᴉɥʇǝɯoS

Clever Card Tricks

There are hundreds, or even thousands, of card tricks. Some are very difficult and need lots of practice. Here are some easy ones which are fun to do. All you need is a pack of ordinary playing cards.

When you are doing card tricks, talk at the same time if you can. It stops people thinking about what you are doing and puzzling out your secrets.

With the Pick a Card tricks, ask the person to look very hard at the chosen card. While they are staring at it, they will not notice what you are doing.

Crazy Card

When you do this trick make the card follow the wand. Move the wand up and down slowly, then quickly, then in little jerks.

The Secret

Hold some cards like this, your fingers towards people watching. Hold your wand over the cards. Then move your thumb up and down. This will move one card.

Reading Finger Trick

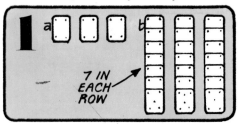

Hold out some cards and ask a friend to pick one (a) without you seeing it. Take it, like this (b) and rub it with one finger. Say you are reading it.

Put the card back in the pack and hold it together neatly (a). Now lift off some cards. The one that comes face up is the card you rubbed with your finger (b).

The secret is that when you rub the card, you bend it a little. When it is in the pack, it holds the cards apart and you can lift them off at the right place every time.

Magic Sevens

This is a really magic trick. It comes right every time you do it but there is no explanation why. You need 21 cards. Any 21 will do but make sure they are all from the same pack.

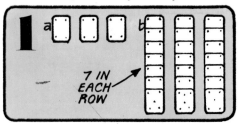

Put down three cards in a line (a). Add a second card to each one in the line, then a third, until you have used them all (b). There will be seven cards in each row.

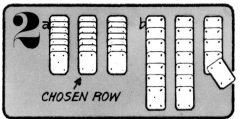

Ask someone to choose a card but keep it a secret. Ask which row the card is in. Pick up that row and put it between the other rows (a). Put out the cards again in the same way in three rows of seven (b).

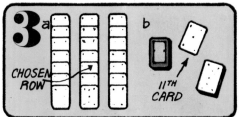

Ask which row the chosen card is now in. Put that row between the other rows (a). Keeping the cards in the same order, turn them over. From the top, count out ten cards. The eleventh is the chosen one.

Why did the chicken cross the road?   For fowl reasons!

Pick A Card

Fan out some cards (a). Ask a friend to pick one and look at it, without you seeing it. Take half the pack in your right hand and look, secretly, at the bottom card (b). Ask a friend to put back the picked card, face down, on the cards in your left hand (c). Put all the cards together. Turn them over, from the top, one at a time. The card after the one you looked at will be the picked card (d).

Pick Another Card

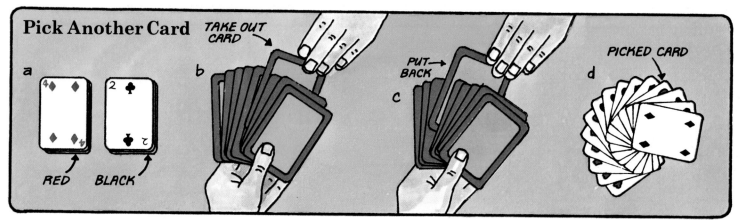

Before you do this trick, divide a pack of cards into red and black ones (a). Put the two halves together again. Fan them out, face down, and ask someone to pick one.

Hold one edge of the fan towards the person so they take a card from one end (a). Ask them to put it back. Move the fan round so it goes in at the other end (b).

Turn the cards over and hold them up so no one else can see them. If the picked card is red, it will be among the black cards. If it is black, it will be with the reds.

1 Card Through Cards

Hold a pack of cards in one hand. Pick off the top two cards, holding the edges exactly together so they look like one card. Let everyone see which card it is.

2

Put the two cards down on top of the pack. Slide off the top one (a) and put it at the bottom of the pack (b). Let everyone see very clearly what you are doing.

3

Give the pack a good bang with one hand (a). Say that this is to bang the bottom card up to the top again. Pick off the top card and show it is the same one again (b).

What do you get if you cross a kangaroo with an elephant? ¡ɐᴉlɐɹʇsn∀ ɹǝʌo llɐ sǝloɥ ǝƃnH

Amazing Water Tricks

Tricky Tumblers

Playing with water is good fun but be careful where you do these tricks. Hold the glass over a big, empty bowl or put a deep tray on top of a table.

Use a thick drinking glass which will not break easily, or better still, an unbreakable one, if you can.

When you do these tricks, turn the glass over as quickly as you can. You will have to practise them a few times first.

1 Clever Cloth

WATER

CLOTH

GLASS

Put a piece of thin cloth over a glass. Let it flop over loosely. Pour in some water, through the cloth, until the glass is full.

2 TURN UPSIDE DOWN VERY QUICKLY

a   b

HOLD TIGHTLY

Stretch the cloth tightly over the glass. Hold it down with one hand. Turn the glass upside down very quickly. Hold it straight and the water will stay in.

1 Sticky Paper

SHEET OF PAPER

GLASS

WATER

Fill up a glass with water, almost to the top. Put a piece of stiff, thick paper over the top of the glass. Hold it down with one hand.

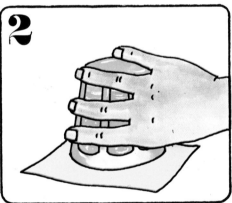

2

Hold the glass with the other hand and turn it over quickly. Take away the hand holding the paper. The paper will stick to the glass and keep the water in.

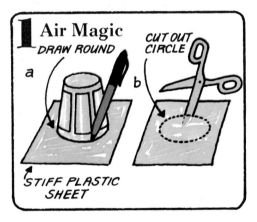

1 Air Magic

DRAW ROUND

CUT OUT CIRCLE

a   b

STIFF PLASTIC SHEET

Put an empty glass down on a sheet of stiff, colourless plastic. Draw round the glass with a ball point pen (a). Cut along the line with scissors (b) to cut out a circle.

2

PLASTIC CIRCLE

To do the trick, hide the plastic circle under the piece of stiff paper. Fill up the glass. Hold the circle under the paper and put it over the top of the glass.

3

Make sure the circle is exactly over the top of the glass. Hold the paper down with one hand and turn the glass over with the other.

4

PEEL OFF PAPER

Peel the paper off very slowly and carefully. The plastic circle will stick and hold the water in. From a little distance, it will look like magic.

When is it bad luck to be followed by a black cat? When you're a mouse!

Coloured Water Magic

This trick will really puzzle people but do not let them come too close when you do it. Practise it a few times first so you get it just right.

You will need a glass with lines or ridges on it, a small square scarf or coloured handkerchief, and some pieces of stiff, coloured plastic or acetate. If you can find lots of different colours, you can make the trick last much longer.

How It Looks

1 Hold up a glass full of coloured water. Drop a bright scarf or handkerchief over it.

HERE IS A GLASS OF GREEN WATER I COVER IT WITH MY MAGIC HANDKERCHIEF.

2 Lift off the scarf and the water has changed colour. Cover the glass and change the colour again.

I LIFT OFF THE HANDKERCHIEF AND THE GREEN WATER HAS TURNED INTO ORANGEADE!

1 Before You Start

STIFF COLOURED PLASTIC   CUT TO FILL

Cut out pieces of coloured plastic so that they just fit tightly in the glass. Cut about 1 cm off the top. Each piece should slide in and out easily but stay upright.

2

THIN NYLON LINE

Make a small hole in the top of each plastic shape. Tie a short piece of nylon line or thin white thread to each shape.

3

WATER

PLASTIC SHAPES

Push all the shapes into the glass so they stand upright. Hang the strings over one side, towards you. Pour in enough water to fill the glass nearly to the top.

1 The Secret

Hold up the glass. Be very careful that the shapes are flat towards the people watching. If they are sideways on, they will show. Drop the scarf over the glass.

2

PICK UP THREAD

With your finger and thumb, pick up a thread through the scarf and lift it up. Hide the shape in the scarf. Cover the glass again and take out another shape.

3

When you have taken out all the shapes, drink the water to show it is real. Or make the trick longer by putting back the shapes. This needs a bit more practice.

What's worse than finding a maggot in an apple? Finding half a maggot!

Crafty Coin Tricks

Vanishing Coin

1 "WATCH THIS CAREFULLY. I'M GOING TO PRESS THIS COIN INTO YOUR HAND THREE TIMES."

Ask a friend to sit down facing you and hold out one hand. Hold a coin between your fingers and thumb. Press it into the friend's hand but keep hold of it.

2 "THE THIRD TIME I WANT YOU TO GRAB IT FROM ME."

Lift your hand above your head. Then press the coin into the hand again. The third time ask the friend to grab it. But the coin has vanished. Show your empty hand.

The Secret

When you raise your hand the third time, drop the coin on to the top of your head. Pretend you are still holding it and press the friend's hand hard with one finger.

Magic Spinner

1 Hold a big coin upright on a table with one finger, like this. Now rub that finger with a finger of the other hand. Explain that you are working up the magic.

2 Now quickly rub your finger along towards the nail. Lift up both hands and the coin spins away.

The Secret

When you do the last rub of your finger, whizz your hand away and just catch the edge of the coin with your thumb. This is to make it spin. Practise it in secret.

Detective Work

1 TOPS

SMALL COIN

Put three small bottle tops, all exactly the same, down on a table. Give someone a small coin and ask him to hide it under one top while you look the other way.

2 When the coin has been hidden, stare very hard at each top. Then pick up the one hiding the coin. You will be right every time.

The Secret

GLUE

HAIR

Before you do this trick, pull out a hair from your head. Glue about 3 cm of it to a coin, like this. When the coin is under a top, look for the hair sticking out under it.

24

What cake tried to conquer the world? Attila the Bun!

Dissolving Coin

1 HERE IS A COIN AND MY MAGIC SCARF.

2 I HIDE THE COIN IN THE SCARF.

3 NOW I PICK UP A GLASS OF WATER.

4 I PUT THE SCARF OVER THE GLASS AND DROP THE COIN IN.

5 I TAKE AWAY THE SCARF AND YOU CAN SEE THE PENNY.

6 I COVER THE GLASS AGAIN WITH THE SCARF AND SAY THE MAGIC WORDS...

7 WHEN I TAKE AWAY THE SCARF THE COIN HAS *DISAPPEARED!*

1 The Secret
DROP COIN
TILT GLASS

When you cover the glass with the scarf, tilt the glass a little. Drop the coin so it hits the outside of the glass and falls into your hand.

2 COIN UNDER THE GLASS

Before you take the scarf away, make sure the coin is under the glass. It will then look as if it is in the glass.

3 COIN HIDDEN IN HAND

When you take away the scarf again, hide the coin in your hand. Hold the glass up with your fingers and thumb. You can put the coin in your pocket or hide it later.

How does an elephant get down from a tree? Stands on a leaf and waits for autumn!

Surprises

This is a very good trick. People can stand quite close without seeing how you do it. But it needs lots of practice. Follow the instructions and do the trick several times in secret to get it right.

Before you start, crumple up four bits of tissue paper into balls. You also need two saucers.

When you do the trick, hold the saucers upside down, with your thumbs on top and fingers underneath. Pick up the paper balls between your fingers so they are hidden under the saucer. Do not turn the saucers over during the trick.

1 "HERE ARE FOUR BALLS OF TISSUE PAPER AND TWO SAUCERS."

Put the four balls on the table in a square, like this. They should be about 20 cm apart. Pick up the two saucers with your thumbs on top and fingers underneath.

2 "I CAN COVER ANY TWO BALLS AT A TIME, LIKE THIS OR ANY OTHER WAY."

Cover two balls with saucers, then two more several times. The last time, secretly pick up ball 1 in your right hand. Slide the left saucer over the empty place. Put the right saucer over ball 2 and drop ball 1.

3 "I COVER TWO BALLS AND PICK UP THE THIRD BALL."

Leave both saucers on the table and pick up ball 3 in your left hand. Pass it to your right hand.

4 "I PUSH THE BALL UP THROUGH THE TABLE AND SAY THE MAGIC WORDS."

Pretend to push ball 3 up through the table. Knock on the underside of the table, pretending it is very hard to get through. Secretly hide the ball in your right hand.

5 "I LIFT UP THE SAUCER AND THERE ARE THE TWO BALLS."

Pick up the saucer in your left hand to show the two balls underneath it. Pass the saucer to your right hand, which is hiding ball 3.

6 "I COVER THE TWO BALLS AND PICK UP THE FOURTH ONE."

Put the saucer in your right hand over the two balls and drop ball 3 beside them. Now pick up ball 4.

7 "I PUSH IT UP THROUGH THE TABLE AND SAY THE MAGIC WORDS. I LIFT UP THE SAUCER AND THERE IT IS."

Pretend to push ball 4 up through the table. Hide it in your right hand. Lift up the saucer with your left hand to show three balls. Pass the saucer to your right hand. Put it over the three balls and drop ball 4 beside them.

8 "I NOW PULL THE LAST BALL DOWN THROUGH THE TABLE AND PUSH IT UP BESIDE THE OTHER THREE. I LIFT UP THE SAUCER AND THERE THEY ARE!"

Put your hand under the table. Pretend to move ball 4 from under the empty saucer and push it up under the other one. Lift up the saucer to show the four balls. Pick up the other saucer to show there is nothing under it.

26 How does a sparrow with engine failure land safely? By sparrowchute!

Night Pinger

This is a good trick to do at night. Put the Pinger in a cupboard in a bedroom or under a bed. It will go on working for a very long time. As the peas take up the hot water, they grow bigger. Then they push out of the cup and drop on to the tray.

You will need
2 plastic cups or pots
a tin tray or big baking tray
a big cardboard box
dried peas or beans
glue

Glue the cups, end to end, like this. Fill the top cup with as many dried peas as you can push in.

Put the tray in the bottom of the cardboard box. Stand the cups on the tray. Pour hot water into the top cup. Close the box and wait very patiently for the pings.

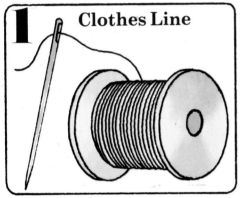

Clothes Line

Push the end of the thread on a reel of coloured cotton through the eye of a big needle.

Push the needle through the sleeve of your jersey or shirt from the inside. Pull off the needle, leaving a bit of thread hanging on the outside.

When someone says "You've got a thread hanging" and pulls it, the thread just gets longer and longer. Make sure the reel can unwind easily but stay hidden.

Cardboard Flapper

Pass the Flapper to a friend or send it in an envelope through the post.

You will need
a big paper clip or piece of
    strong, bendy wire,
    about 12 cm long
a rubber band
a strip of cardboard,
    about 12 cm long and
    8 cm wide
a small square of thick
    cardboard
sticky tape

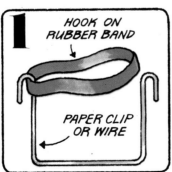

Bend the paper clip or wire into this shape. Bend over the two ends. Hook the rubber band across the top.

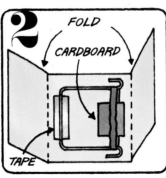

Fold the cardboard in three, like this. Stick one side of the clip to the middle fold of the cardboard. Slide the small cardboard square between the band.

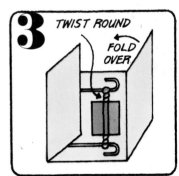

Wind the cardboard square round and round about 20 times. Fold over the two flaps of the cardboard strip to stop the square unwinding. The Flapper is ready.

What do you get if you cross a mink with a kangaroo? A fur coat with big pockets!

Putting on a Show

When you are good at doing magic, try putting on a show for your friends. On the next four pages are things you can make before a show. You can use most of the other tricks in this book as well.

Before a show, practise all the tricks lots of times in front of a mirror. Then you can see exactly how they look.

Write out a list of your tricks and put it on the table. It will remind you in which order you have decided to do them. Put all the things you need on the table. Have a box beside it so you can drop things into it when you have done the tricks. Start and end the show with two of your very best tricks. Arrange the others so each one looks very different from the last. Do not do two which look a bit alike.

If you find it easy, talk to the audience while you are doing the tricks. If this is hard for you, put on a record or radio music programme, just loud enough for people to hear.

It is a good idea to have an assistant to help you and hand you the things you need. Choose a friend who will keep your magic tricks a secret.

Making Mistakes

When you are putting on a show, don't worry if a trick goes wrong. Just pretend it is part of the show and no one will notice. It is a good idea to have a whistle or something which makes a noise. This startles the audience and you can go on to the next trick. Or you can do a quick trick. Here are two you can have ready if you need to cover up a mistake.

LIGHT

ASSISTANT →

BOX FOR DONE TRICKS

LIST OF TRICKS

You will need a table to do your tricks on. Cover it with a cloth if you have one. Before the show arrange the chairs for the audience. Make sure everyone sits in front of the table and not too close to it. If you can, put a light near the front of the table and just to one side. The light should not be too bright.

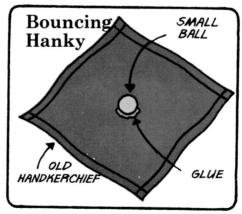

Bouncing Hanky — SMALL BALL — OLD HANDKERCHIEF — GLUE

Glue a small ball to the middle of a handkerchief. Pull out the hanky. Pretend to wipe your face and drop it on the floor. It will bounce back up to your hand.

Big Sneeze — HANDKERCHIEF — BIG JAGGED HOLE — SNIFF

Cut a large jagged hole in an old hanky. Pull it out of a pocket and pretend to sneeze into it. Hold it up show how strong your sneeze was.

Doctor, doctor, I've got only 59 seconds to live. Hold on, I'll be with you in a minute

Magic Boxes

You can use this magic box for making all sorts of things appear – or disappear – by magic.

You will need

a cardboard box about 28 cm long, 16 cm wide and 8 cm deep

a piece of cardboard the same size as the lid of the box

a piece of cardboard the same size as the end of the box

a piece of black card, or card painted black, the same length as the box and about 5 cm wider

2 elastic bands

4 paper fasteners

paints, sticky tape and scissors

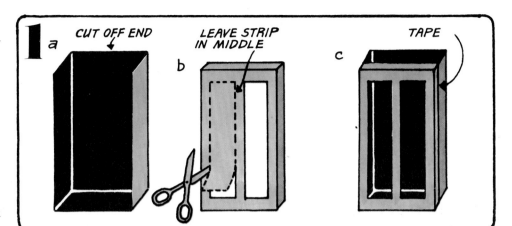

Cut one end off the box (a). Paint the inside black. Cut two long strips out of the lid, leaving a strip down the middle (b).

Put the lid on the box. Stick it down all the way round the edges with tape (c).

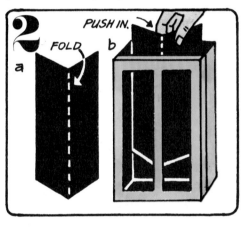

Fold the piece of black cardboard in half, lengthways (a). Push it into the box, like this (b). This makes a secret space at the back of the box.

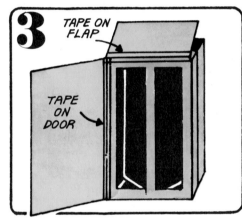

Stick the large piece of cardboard to the side of the box with tape to make a door. Stick the smaller piece of cardboard to the top of the box to make a flap.

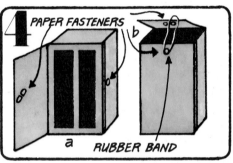

Push a paper fastener through the door and another through the side of the box (a). Push a third fastener through the flap and a fourth through the box back (b).

Hook a rubber band over the door fastener and the side one. Hook a band over the flap and back fasteners.

Put small scarves, handkerchiefs or lots of small flat things into the secret space in the box. Close the door and the flap. Hook up the rubber bands.

Unhook the rubber bands. Open the door and show people the inside of the box. Put your hand into the space in the front to prove that the box is empty.

Close the door and hook up the band. Say the magic words or wave your wand. Open the flap and slowly pull out the things you have hidden in the back.

What do you call a strange thing which falls into a chip pan? An unidentified frying object!

Magic Balls

This trick needs quite a lot of practice or people may see how you do it.

Use strong, thin black or brown thread. If you can get it, colourless nylon thread is best.

If the box is thin cardboard, tear it up at the end to prove there are no balls in it.

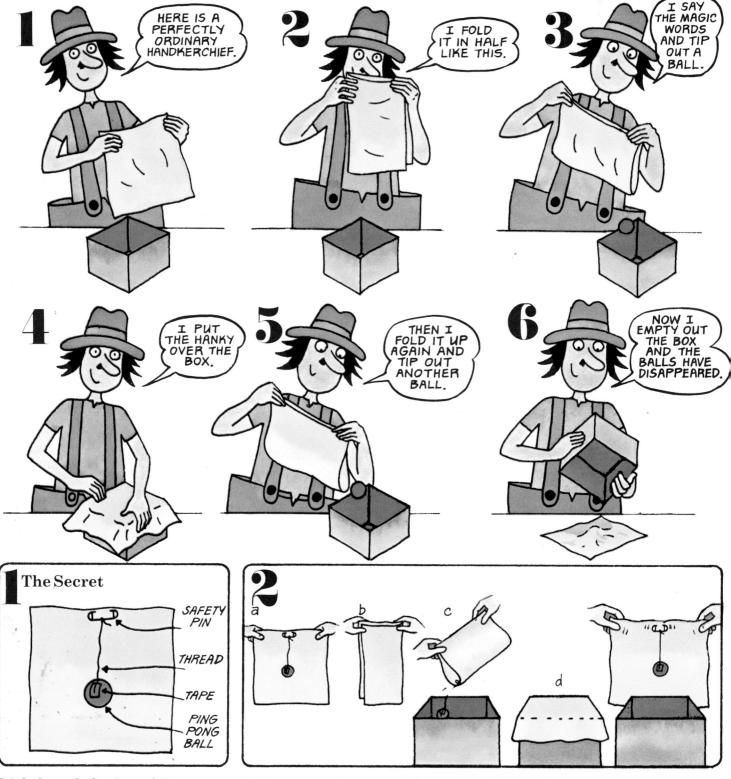

1 HERE IS A PERFECTLY ORDINARY HANDKERCHIEF.

2 I FOLD IT IN HALF LIKE THIS.

3 I SAY THE MAGIC WORDS AND TIP OUT A BALL.

4 I PUT THE HANKY OVER THE BOX.

5 THEN I FOLD IT UP AGAIN AND TIP OUT ANOTHER BALL.

6 NOW I EMPTY OUT THE BOX AND THE BALLS HAVE DISAPPEARED.

1 The Secret

SAFETY PIN
THREAD
TAPE
PING PONG BALL

Stick the end of a piece of thin, strong thread to a ping pong ball with tape. Tie the other end to a safety pin. Put the safety pin in the hem of a big handkerchief.

2
a b c d

Hold up the hanky with the ball towards you (a). Fold it in half (b). Tip out the ball into the box (c). Let the hanky fall over the box (d).

Pick up the two corners nearest you so the ball is still towards you (e). You can tip out the ball in the same way lots of times. Then show the box is empty.

30

What do you do to a blue banana? Cheer it up!

Magic Tubes

You can make lots of things appear out of these magic tubes. Remember to pull a tube down when you are taking one off. And push it up from the bottom when you are putting it on again.

You will need

a small tin without a lid

2 sheets of thin cardboard or thick paper, big enough to roll round the tin

a paper clip and sticky tape

coloured ribbons or long strips of thin, coloured paper

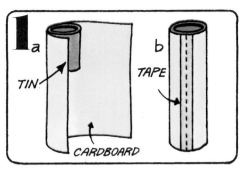

Put the tin down on a sheet of cardboard or paper (a). Roll the sheet loosely round the tin to make a tube. Stick the edge with tape (b).

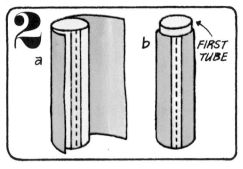

Roll the tube up in the second sheet of cardboard to make another tube. Stick the edge with tape. The first tube should slide easily inside the second one.

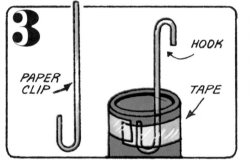

Straighten out one end of a paper clip. Stick the loop end to the top edge of a tin with tape, like this. Bend over the straight end to make a small hook.

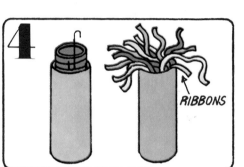

Slide the first tube into the second one. Put the tin into the top of the tubes. Make sure the paper clip hooks on to them. Fill the tin with ribbons or long strips of paper.

The Secret

Keep the hook towards you. Hold the outside tube and slide the inside one downwards. Show that it is empty. Now slide it up inside the outside tube. Hold the inside tube at the top and slide the outside one downwards. Show that it is empty. Slide it on again from the bottom. Hold both tubes in one hand and pull the ribbons out of the tin.

How It Looks

What do you get if you cross an elephant with a mouse? Huge holes in the skirting boards!

Grand Finisher

This is a very good trick to do as the last one in a show. You need a helper ready in the audience. He should pretend he does not know what you are going to do. Before you start this trick, ask for a volunteer from the audience. Your helper must get up very quickly before anyone else offers to help.

A few days before the show, find an old shirt for your helper to wear. Write in big letters, with a brush and paint, 'The End' across the back of the shirt. Leave the paint to dry.

1 I AM NOW GOING TO TAKE OFF THIS VOLUNTEER'S SHIRT. FIRST I UNDO THE BUTTONS ON HIS COLLAR AND SHIRT FRONT.

Ask your helper to sit down on a chair or stool. Stand behind him and undo the buttons on his shirt collar and shirt front.

2 I NOW UNDO THE BUTTONS ON HIS CUFFS.

Now undo the buttons on your helper's shirt sleeves.

3 I SAY THE MAGIC WORDS AND GIVE THE SHIRT A GOOD PULL.

Take hold of the shirt collar. Say the magic words. Give the shirt a good pull upwards.

4 I SAY SOME MORE MAGIC WORDS AND OFF COMES THE SHIRT!

Say some more magic words. Pull the shirt again. Keep on pulling and it will come right off from under the helper's coat.

5 THE END

Turn the shirt round so the audience can see what is written on the back. Everyone will then know the show is over and will clap while you bow.

The Secret

1

Before the show, put the shirt round your helper, so that it hangs down his back. Do not put his arms into the shirt sleeves.

2

Do up the collar button and the top two front buttons. Put the sleeves down his arms and do up the buttons.

3

Put on the helper's coat and do up the buttons. Make sure that the shirt looks as if it is on properly and that sleeve ends show under the coat.

What do you get if you pour boiling water down a rabbit hole?   A hot cross bunny!